FAIRY TALE TIME

Illustrated by Gerry Embleton and
Gill Embleton

BRIMAX·NEWMARKET·ENGLAND

The Hare and the Tortoise

A hare came leaping across the field. He loved darting this way and that, stopping to look and listen, then to be off again as fast as he could go.

He was at the hedge, nosing his way through into a grassy lane when he saw the tortoise. Hare sat up on his strong hind legs, ears held high and his whiskers twitching. He always laughed at Tortoise – that heavy shell, the funny wrinkled face and neck poking out in front, and those bent legs! . . . How could anyone walk on such legs?

"Poor old Tortoise," he chuckled. "He is so slow . . . Slow as a snail!"

Then he called:

"Hallo there, Tortoise! . . . Are you walking your slowest or your fastest?"

"Always at the same pace, Hare," the tortoise replied. "Just slow but sure."

"There's one thing for sure," teased the hare, "you'll always be the last getting there – wherever it might be!"

"Oh, I don't know," Tortoise answered in his calm, thoughtful way. "I think we should have a race. I will win of course."

This amused the hare so much he was quite doubled up with laughter.

"Do you . . . mean that?" he choked, trying to take a deep breath.

"Of course! I always mean what I say," said the tortoise.

A fox was peeping from behind a tree, listening and grinning with delight at what he heard.

'This will be fun,' he thought and came forward hoping to take part in some way.

"Good morning, gentlemen! . . . Can I help? . . . Get things going, perhaps?" he asked.

All the woodland animals stood by chatting and waiting to see the race.

When they'd agreed on how far to go and which tree should be the winning post, the hare and the tortoise stood ready at the starting line.

Fox gave the signal . . . They were off!

The hare bounded away and reached the top of the next hill in no time at all. There he stopped to look back.

"Poor old Tortoise," he said to himself, "not even in sight . . . Beat me indeed! . . . I might as well have a rest."

So, he settled down in the cool grass and fell fast asleep.

Meanwhile, the tortoise plodded on; step by step, never looking round, never stopping. He just kept doing what he'd made up his mind to do. Fox saw it all and smiled.

The other animals took a short cut across the field and were there at the post to watch for the winner.

It was a very hot day. The sun began to burn the hare's nose and so he woke up. The fox, waiting behind the hedge, turned and made a dash for the finishing line.

Hare sat up, rubbing his eyes, wondering what he was doing there.

"Oh yes, of course, the race," he mumbled. "Where's poor old Tortoise now?" and he glanced down the lane. There was no sign of those funny little legs. Hare looked the other way; the lane was empty.

"Ah well, I'd better push on. . . . I'll give him a wave as I pass," and Hare giggled to think of it.

There was the winning post, round the next bend, and everybody was jumping up and down with excitement.

'How nice!' Hare thought. 'My friends have come to cheer me.' Then he heard the words, "Come on, Tortoise . . . Only a few steps . . . That's it! . . . You've WON! . . . Good old Tortoise!"

Hare arrived feeling very foolish.

"How did you manage it, Tortoise?" everyone was asking.

"Well, slow and steady wins the race," he replied and started nibbling a juicy leaf.

I don't think Hare teased him any more – do you?

9

The Enormous Turnip

Old Mr Poppascoff walked around his garden looking at his flowers and vegetables growing there. Then he saw the turnip!

"Come here, quickly," he called to his wife. "I only planted this yesterday. You can almost see it growing as you watch it."

"I don't like it," she whispered. "It's not right . . . it seems very strange to me."

Mr Poppascoff patted the turnip. "Now don't grow any more today . . . I'll come and see you in the morning."

Early the next morning, they woke to find the sun streaming in through the bedroom window. It was a lovely pale green. Mr Poppascoff padded over to the window in his bare feet.

"Oh dear!" he muttered. "Oh, my goodness me!" His wife came to see what he was looking at. She had to stand on tiptoe, as the floor was very cold.

"That wretched turnip!" she cried. "I knew there was something wrong as soon as I saw it."

They went down into the garden to have a look at it. The turnip was enormous. They fell over backwards, just trying to see the top and there they sat, staring up at it.

10

"Whatever shall we do?" wailed Mrs Poppascoff.

"Eat it, I hope," said her husband. He went to fetch a ladder and a saw to cut it down.

Up and up he climbed, while his wife held the ladder. Then, standing on the turnip top, he worked around, sawing the stalks off. Mrs Poppascoff sank beneath the falling leaves and was quite buried. She was not at all pleased.

After Mr Poppascoff had rescued her, they dragged all the leaves away. Then he tied one end of a rope round the stumps that were left and one end around his waist.

"Now, my dear," he said, "you push the turnip from that side. I will pull from this . . . we'll soon have it over."

But the turnip just wouldn't move.

"We'll both pull," said his wife.

So they pulled. Still the turnip wouldn't move.

Children coming home from school stopped to watch.

"Hi! . . . Johnny!" called Mr Poppascoff. "Come and help us pull up this turnip."

"Right," cried Johnny and he grabbed the old woman round her waist. They all pulled.

But still the turnip wouldn't move.

11

Johnny called to Sally, his sister, so she came to help.
"Pull!" cried Mr Poppascoff . . . "and again!"

They dug in their heels, they got red in the face, but try as hard as they could, nothing would move the turnip.

"Call the dog," Johnny said. So Mr Poppascoff whistled for Bess, the dog. She too, helped to pull. Still the turnip would not move.

Then, Tabitha the cat, came and held on to the dog's tail.

"This time we'll do it," cried the old man. . . . "Ready, steady, Pull! Pull as hard as you can!"

But still the turnip would not move.

Suddenly, a little mouse raced across the garden. Down went Tabitha's paw, right across the mouse's tail.

"You live here doing nothing for your keep," said the cat. "Now get under that turnip and nibble through it, before I nibble you! . . . Then come and help to pull."

So the little mouse did just as he was told. Then he twisted his tail round the cat's tail and he started to pull.

Once! Twice! . . . they pulled. Dirt and grit fell down on them like a shower of hailstones. Then all at once, the turnip shot out from the ground.

Everyone fell over in a heap! The little mouse pulled his tail away from the cat and ran. He didn't want to be squashed or nibbled.

Mr Poppascoff invited them all to supper.

"Bring your friends," he cried. "Bring everyone . . . You'll love my wife's turnip soup."

What a party! Everyone came and all the visitors had plenty to eat.

When they had gone, Bess and Tabitha lay snoozing on the mat, the little mouse was curled up in his hole and Mr Poppascoff and his wife sat watching the fire.

"It was a good party," said the old man.

"Very good," his wife agreed.

"No one could do better than that," he said. "Or grow such a turnip," he added. "I've never seen one like it before and there's plenty left."

"I don't want to see another turnip as long as I live!" cried the old woman. "I'm sick of turnips."

Silence . . . even the clock had stopped ticking. Slowly the old man turned to look at her.

"My dear, you can't mean that . . . whatever is wrong with seeing turnips? They are quite beautiful . . . but as long as I live I'll never EAT ANOTHER."

Mr Poppascoff and his wife fell back in their chairs. They laughed till the tears ran down their cheeks. The animals grinned, the clock ticked again and the fire sparkled once more in the grate.

Snow White and the Seven Dwarfs

Once there was a little princess whose skin was white as snow, whose cheeks were red as roses, and whose hair was black as ebony. Her name was Snow White. She had a stepmother who was beautiful and very vain. Every day she would look into her magic mirror and ask:—

"Mirror, mirror, on the wall, who is the fairest of us all?"

The mirror always answered that the Queen was, until one fateful day, when it replied,

"Thou Queen art fair and beauteous to see, But Snow White is fairer far than thee."

The Queen was so angry she called a servant and ordered him to take Snow White to the forest, and kill her.

The servant loved Snow White. He could not kill her, but when he returned from the forest he told the Queen he had obeyed her order, for he knew she would send someone else to do the deed if she knew Snow White was still alive.

Snow White wandered alone through the forest until she came to a small cottage. Inside, everything was arranged in sevens. She was so hungry she couldn't resist taking a small bite from each of the seven pieces of bread set upon seven plates on the wooden table.

And then, because she was tired, she lay on one of the seven beds and fell asleep. She was found by the seven dwarfs, who owned the cottage, when they returned from a day's digging at the mines.

They took pity on Snow White when she told them her story and said she could stay with them.

The following day, the wicked Queen asked her magic mirror who was the fairest in the land.

"Queen, thou art of beauty rare," it replied,
"But Snow White living in the glen
With the seven little men,
Is a thousand times more fair."

The Queen was very angry because she knew her servant had deceived her. She quickly dressed herself as a pedlar and went to the dwarfs cottage.

"Will you buy a pretty petticoat, child?" she asked Snow White, who alas, did not recognise her.

The wicked Queen slipped the petticoat over Snow White's head and pulled the tapes so tightly round her waist that Snow White stopped breathing. The dwarfs found her lying on the floor when they got home. At first they thought she was dead, but when they saw the tight lace they guessed what had happened and loosened it, and Snow White began to breathe again.

The Queen thought she had killed Snow White. When the magic mirror said that Snow White was still the fairest in the land she turned white with rage. She dressed herself in a different disguise and hastened to the dwarfs' cottage with a poisoned comb in her pedlar's basket. It was so pretty that Snow White could not resist trying it in her hair. The instant it touched her head she fell to the floor.

When the dwarfs came home they took the comb from her hair and revived her.

"You must not speak to anyone." they said. "The wicked Queen is trying to kill you."

When the magic mirror told the Queen that Snow White was still the fairest in the land she determined to kill her or die herself in the attempt. This time she took a poisoned apple to the cottage.

Alas, Snow White forgot the dwarf's warning, and took a bite from the apple.

This time, the dwarfs could not revive her.

This time, the magic mirror replied to the Queen:—

"Thou Queen are the fairest in all the land."

16

The dwarfs laid Snow White in a crystal case in a forest glade, and kept watch over her day and night, for they had grown to love her.

One day a Prince came riding by. When he saw Snow White, whose skin was still as white as snow, whose cheeks were still as red as roses, whose hair was still as black as ebony, he pleaded with the dwarfs to let him take her home to his palace. The Prince looked so sad when they refused that the dwarfs changed their minds, and agreed to his request. And then, just as the Prince was lifting Snow White onto his horse, the piece of apple, which unbeknown to anyone had been lodged in her throat, fell from her mouth, and she opened her eyes.

The wicked Queen could not believe it when her mirror said:—
"Oh Queen, although you are of beauty rare,
The Prince's bride is a thousand times more fair."

When she saw that Snow White was the Prince's bride, she choked with rage . . . and died.

Now Snow White had nothing to fear from the wicked Queen and she lived happily with her Prince, and visited the seven little dwarfs as often as she could.

Goldilocks and the Three Bears

Once there were three bears. A father bear, a mother bear and a baby bear.

One morning Mother Bear made the porridge for breakfast as usual. "The porridge is exceedingly hot this morning," said Mother Bear.

"Let us go for a stroll in the wood while it cools," said Father Bear.

There was someone else walking in the wood that morning. A little girl with long golden hair, called Goldilocks. She could smell the beautiful aroma of porridge and she followed it, her nose twitching, until she came to the open window of the Bears' house. When she saw the three bowls of steaming porridge on the table they made her feel so hungry she climbed in through the window without so much as a 'please may I?'

"I think I'll try some of that," she said. She tried the porridge in the large bowl first. It was so hot it burnt her tongue.

"Ouch!" she said, and dropped the spoon.

The porridge in the middle size bowl was far too sweet.

"Ugh!" she said, and dropped that spoon too.

The porridge in the small bowl was just the way she liked it.

"Ooh lovely!" she said, and ate it all up.

When the small bowl was quite, quite empty she walked around the house opening cupboards, and looking at this, and looking at that, and trying everything she could see.

She sat on Father Bear's big chair.

"Oh no . . ." she said, "This is much too hard."

She sat on Mother Bear's middle size chair.

"Oh no . . ." she said, "This is much too soft."

She sat on Baby Bear's chair.

"Ooh lovely!" she said. "This is so comfortable."

But she wriggled and fidgeted about so much that one of the legs snapped in two and she fell to the floor.

She picked herself up and went into the bear's bedroom.

She tried Father Bear's big bed.

"Oh no . . ." she said. "This is much too bumpy."

She tried Mother Bear's middle size bed.

"Oh no . . ." she said, "This is much too squashy."

She tried Baby Bear's small bed.

"Ooh lovely!" she said, "This is so comfortable." And she fell fast asleep with her head on Baby Bear's pillow.

When the bears got home they could tell at once that someone had been inside their house.

"Who has been eating my porridge?" growled Father Bear.

"Who has been eating my porridge?" growled Mother Bear.

"And who has been eating my porridge, and finished it all up?" squeaked Baby Bear.

"Who has been sitting on my chair?" growled Father Bear.

"Who has been sitting on my chair?" growled Mother Bear.

"And who has been sitting on my chair, and broken it?" squeaked Baby Bear and he burst into tears.

"Who has been lying on my bed?" growled Father Bear.
"Who has been lying on my bed?" growled Mother Bear.
"Someone has been lying on my bed and she is still here." squeaked Baby Bear. "LOOK!"

Goldilocks opened her eyes and sat up. When she saw the three bears staring at her she jumped off the bed and out through the window so quickly the bears were taken by surprise.

The bears didn't bother to chase after her. She looked so frightened they knew she had learned her lesson and would never go uninvited into someone else's house again.

Instead, Mother Bear made some more porridge for Baby Bear. Father Bear mended his chair. And then they all sat down and had breakfast.

Jack and the Beanstalk

Jack lived with his mother in a tumble down house. They were so poor they never seemed to have enough to eat, and one day, Jack's mother said,

"Jack, you must take the cow to market and sell her."

"If I do that we will have no milk," said Jack.

"If we don't sell her we will soon have nothing to eat at all," replied his mother.

And so, very sadly, Jack led the cow to market. He was about half way there when he met an old man.

"Is your cow for sale?" asked the old man. Jack said that she was.

"Then I'll give you five beans for her," said the old man.

Jack laughed.

"You can't buy a cow with five beans," he said.

"Ah," said the old man, "But these are magic beans. You will make a fortune with them."

Jack couldn't resist such a good bargain. He gave the cow an affectionate pat, handed her halter to the old man, and took the five beans in exchange.

Jack's mother was furious.
"We needed money to buy
food," she scolded. "How could
you be so stupid?" She snatched
the beans from Jack's hand and
tossed them out of the window.

"That's what I think of
your bargain," she said.

Jack went sadly to bed,
without any supper. He supposed
he had been rather silly. He
would have to go in search of
work the following day for he
couldn't let his mother starve.

Next morning he woke up
bright and early. Instead of the
bright rays of sunlight which
usually lay across his bedroom
floor, there was a large shadow.
He went to the window to see
what was blocking out the sun.
Growing from the ground below
his window was the biggest
beanstalk in the world. It
reached up . . . up . . . up into the
sky and the top of it was lost
among the clouds.

"The old man was right,
they were magic beans," he said,
"I'm going to climb to the top to
see what I can find."

Jack's mother begged him
not to go, but Jack had made up
his mind.

He climbed and climbed, up

and up. He climbed through white swirling clouds until he came to the very tip of the beanstalk, and from the top of the beanstalk he stepped into another land. It was a land just like his own except that everything in it was twice and three times as big. All the climbing had made him hungry, so he went to the door of the only house he could see and knocked boldly. The door was opened by a huge woman. She was so big she was surely the wife of a giant. Jack persuaded her to give him some breakfast. He had just finished eating when he heard footsteps as heavy as falling boulders and then a voice as loud as thunder.

"FEE FI FO FUM, I SMELL THE BLOOD OF AN ENGLISHMAN!"

Quick as a flash, the giant woman bundled Jack into the oven.

"Sh . . . be very quiet," she said, "That's my husband. He eats boys like you for breakfast."

The huge woman, who was indeed the wife of a giant, told her husband he was mistaken and put a bowl of porridge on the table.

When he had eaten, the giant called for his hen.

"Lay!" he ordered. And the hen lay a golden egg.

Jack, who could see everything that was happening through a crack in the oven door, determined to have that hen for himself.

Presently the giant's head began to nod. Soon he was asleep. As quick as a bee about to sting, Jack left the oven, picked up the hen, ran to the top of the beanstalk and climbed down to earth again.

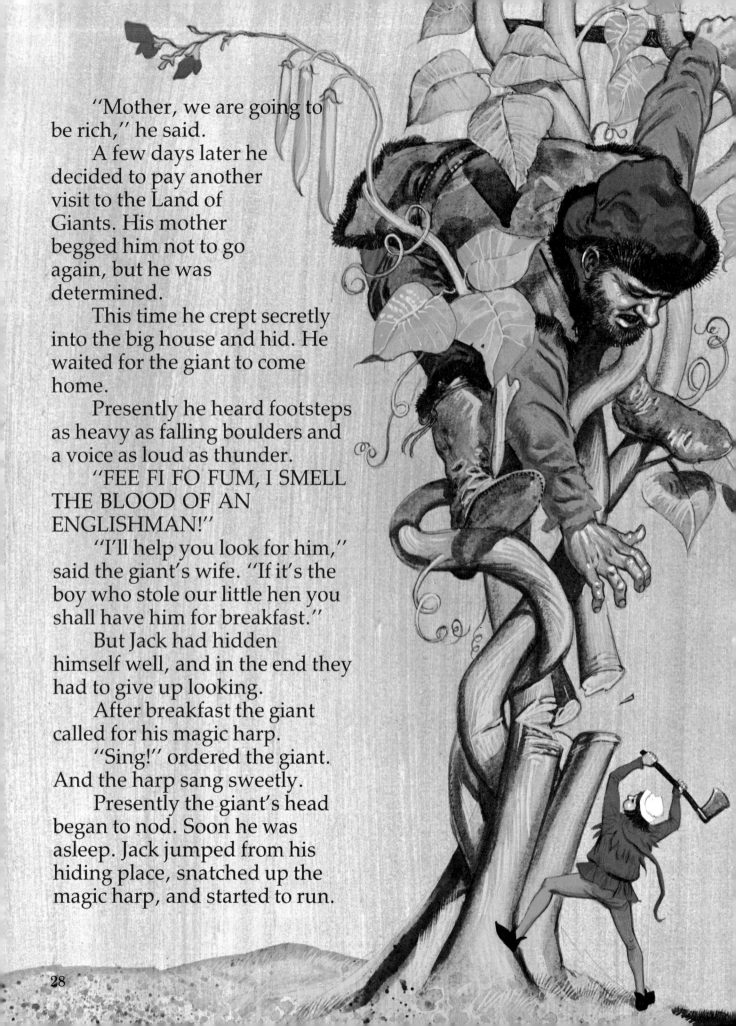

"Mother, we are going to be rich," he said.

A few days later he decided to pay another visit to the Land of Giants. His mother begged him not to go again, but he was determined.

This time he crept secretly into the big house and hid. He waited for the giant to come home.

Presently he heard footsteps as heavy as falling boulders and a voice as loud as thunder.

"FEE FI FO FUM, I SMELL THE BLOOD OF AN ENGLISHMAN!"

"I'll help you look for him," said the giant's wife. "If it's the boy who stole our little hen you shall have him for breakfast."

But Jack had hidden himself well, and in the end they had to give up looking.

After breakfast the giant called for his magic harp.

"Sing!" ordered the giant. And the harp sang sweetly.

Presently the giant's head began to nod. Soon he was asleep. Jack jumped from his hiding place, snatched up the magic harp, and started to run.

"Master! Master!" called the magic harp.

The giant woke with such a roar that the people in the land below the beanstalk thought the sky was falling in.

"FEE FI FO FUM . . ." he bellowed. "I *DO* SMELL THE BLOOD OF AN ENGLISHMAN . . ."

He ran after Jack with great lumbering, thundering steps. Jack was small and nimble, and had a good start. When he reached the top of the beanstalk he tucked the harp inside his shirt and began to climb down.

The beanstalk began to shake, and creak, and groan, as the angry giant followed him . . .

Faster went Jack . . . faster . . . and faster . . .

"Mother!. . ." he called as he neared the bottom. "Bring me an axe . . . quickly . . ."

He jumped to the ground and took the axe. He swung his arms as though he were the strongest man in the world, and with three hefty cuts the beanstalk came tumbling to the ground. There was a terrible roar as the giant fell. He made a hole so big, when he hit the ground, that both he and the beanstalk disappeared into it, and were lost forever.

As for Jack and his mother . . . well, they lived happily ever after with the hen who laid golden eggs, and the harp which sang beautiful songs. They were never poor again.

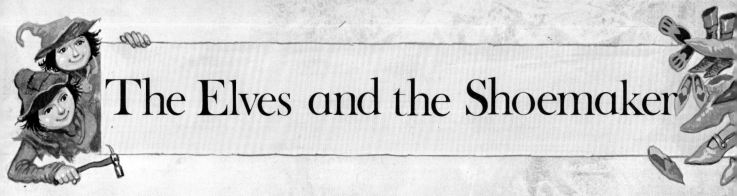

The Elves and the Shoemaker

Once there was a shoemaker. He worked hard, but times were hard and the day came when he was left with just enough leather to make one pair of shoes. He cut the pieces very carefully. One mistake, and there wouldn't have been enough leather to make even one pair. He put the pieces on the bench so that he could begin stitching them together the next morning and went to bed.

During the night, as he and his wife slept, something very mysterious happened.

"Wife! Come quickly!" he called when he went to start work next day.

On the bench, where the pieces of shoe leather had been, was now as fine a pair of finished shoes as they had ever seen.

"How could that have happened?" gasped his wife.

"We must have a friend," said the shoemaker. "And look how well they are made. I couldn't have made them better myself."

He sold the shoes that very morning, and for a very good price. Now he could buy enough leather to make two pairs of shoes. He cut the pieces and left them on his bench as he had done the previous night. When he came down to breakfast the following morning there were four finished shoes on the bench. And so it continued, night after night, after night. The more leather he was able to buy the more shoes he was able to cut. The more pieces he left on his bench, the more finished shoes he found in the morning. The more finished shoes he found, the more leather he was able to buy. It wasn't long before he began to grow rich for the shoes were so beautifully made everyone wanted to own a pair.

One evening, not long before Christmas, his wife said, "I wish we knew who was making the shoes so that we could thank them." The shoemaker wished the same thing himself, and they decided, there and then, that instead of going to bed that night they would stay up and keep watch.

At midnight the door opened and two elves came into the shop. They sat cross-legged on the bench and worked hard and diligently till all the pieces of leather had been sewn into shoes, and then they left, as quietly as they had arrived.

The shoemaker and his wife crept from their hiding place.

Naturally, they were astonished by what they had seen, but try as they would, they could think of no way of thanking the fairy-cobblers until the wife said,

"Did you notice how ragged their clothes were? I will make them each a new suit."

The shoemaker jumped to his feet and said,

"Did you notice that their feet were bare? I will make them both a pair of shoes."

The shoemaker and his wife were so pleased with their idea that they set to work the very next day. By Christmas Eve they had finished. The shoemaker had made four tiny shoes from the softest leather he could buy. His wife had made two pairs of tiny green breeches, two elegant green coats and two tiny frilled shirts, two pairs of white ribbed stockings which she had knitted on darning needles and two jaunty caps each trimmed with a mottled feather. They had taken as much care with their work as the elves had with theirs.

That night, instead of laying the pieces of shoe leather on the work bench they set out the new clothes. And then they hid and kept watch. At the stroke of midnight the two elves crept into the shop. When they saw the two sets of clothes they shouted with delight and threw down their shoemaking tools.

"We need make shoes no more," they sang, as they pulled on their white stockings. They danced from the shop dressed from tip to toe in their new clothes, as happy as any two elves could possibly be.

"How pleased they were," said the shoemaker as he hugged his wife.

"How elegant they looked," said the wife as she hugged the shoemaker.

The shoemaker and his wife never saw the elves again. But their luck had changed and the shoes the shoemaker made sold just as well as the shoes the elves made, and he and his wife prospered and were happy ever after.